The Mountain Whippoorwill

(OR, HOW HILL-BILLY JIM WON THE GREAT FIDDLERS' PRIZE)

BY
STEPHEN VINCENT BENET
(1898-1943)

AS TOLD BY
John McEuen

ILLUSTRATED BY JAS INGRAM AND BUDDY FINETHY
EDITED BY DAVID LANE

This book is dedicated to my daughter, Noel.
She thought it would be a 'good idea' to get Buddy Finethy
involved in doing artwork, and set up a meeting.
Buddy introduced me to Jas Ingram and David Lane,
artists and producers of books and artwork.
They jumped in and did a fine job for The Mountain Whippoorwill,
a poem I have performed for over 50 years.
Whew. We got it done. I will always feel indebted to
all who participated in this project of mine,
this 'adult children's book', something for the fans
from earlier years to read to their grandkids.
Thank you Buddy, Jas, David...
and my favorite daughter, Noel!

www.johnmceuen.net

INTRODUCTION

It was in high school a couple of seniors separately met Hillbilly Jim, from the English book *Adventures in American Literature*. I was drawn to the rhythm and story of how this 'hillbilly' won Essex County Fair's great fiddler's prize. Steve Martin had learned to recite it, and I played the banjo behind him. One night, at a 1965 Orange County concert, the auditorium was dead silent when we finished it. For about 6 long seconds. Then the room exploded; it became the first standing ovation I ever saw. We were both about 19 years old.

I recorded us that week for an 8mm film using Whippoorwill as the soundtrack for my college Art History Class 'term paper'. It got an A+++, saving me from an F.

Steve dropped it from his show, and I took it on – (it was 'his', first). By the mid-'70's I made it a 'B' side of Battle of New Orleans, a NGDB single, and it made it to a Juke box in my 'home town' of Idaho Springs, which I frequented for breakfast, mainly to play it.

One 1970's NGDB opening for John Denver, when I finished Whippoorwill the noise the standing ovation crowd made was such Denver asked me 'where did you get that story?" He wanted to do it. I told him I wrote the music and the poem was Public Domain, but if he did it, I would have to drop it. I remember him walking off saying *"sure a fine piece of material..."*. He never did it.

Years later, at Kevin Nealon's 50th birthday party, I saw Brooke Shields and asked Kevin for an introduction. When he started to introduce me, "Oh, I know this man, Kevin!" she said. "Someone had given me a copy of Mt. Whippoorwill. I was living in New York, modeling, and taking 20 units at college. I couldn't go out at the end of the day; I went to sleep listening to it... it was a great escape; it took me away." I asked "why didn't you call?" She laughed, and we exchanged autographs.

55 years later I played Calhoun, Ga., (where Benet was inspired to write Whippoorwill). That was a great night; taking it around the country for years – I now took it home.

Thanks to my daughter. Noel, she brought me Buddy Finethy, Jas Ingram, David Lane – and their idea of illustrating the book you now hold in your hands. I hope you catch me with my banjo and fiddle, and let me take you away to that time that Mr. Benet's story captured so well.

John McEuen
April, 2024

FOREWORD

I was a mediocre high school student in California when, in English class, the teacher played a vinyl disc of various recorded poetry. One of the poems that stood out was "The Mountain Whippoorwill" by Stephen Vincent Benét. Delivered with a rhythmic bounce, it conveyed the story of a home-grown fiddle contest won by an underdog. The cadence of the poem reflected the various fiddle tunes played during the event, and I was wowed as a sixteen-year-old, having never heard anything like it. Also, I loved its message: victory of soul over style.

Later, on the cusp of leaving my teens, I was desperately searching for material to put in my fledgling – and extremely eclectic – stage show. Already rambling over the fields of magic, juggling, comedy, poetry readings (mostly Carl Sandburg with T. S. Eliot thrown in), and banjo playing, the show might be enhanced, I thought, by the addition of "The Mountain Whippoorwill." I bore down and started memorizing the lengthy poem. I gave it a go at the local club. It was well received, so I incorporated it into my act.

I wanted to use the banjo as a background musical accompaniment but found that playing at the same time as reciting the complex poem was beyond me. John, my high school banjo buddy, who generously gave me my first lessons on the five-string, suggested he could play behind me, giving the poem the mountain music sound that the piece cried out for. The result played well with John's fine banjo background, and I even got a nice review for it in a local free weekly newspaper. John tells me it was the first standing ovation he ever saw.

Eventually, as my act veered toward comedy, the poetry section of my show seemed out of place. I reluctantly dumped the poems and moved toward the goofy. John had recognized the effectiveness of "The Mountain Whippoorwill." He asked if he could appropriate it for his own show, which was founded much more in music than was mine. "I don't own it," was my reply, and I thought it would be great for John's increasingly profound stage show.

John cultivated the piece, adding flowing banjo riffs – unlike me, John was able to play and recite at the same time – and it became an audience-captivating performance piece that has been a staple in his show ever since, with a few hiatuses for retirement and growth. This book is a salute to John's development of the piece and to Stephen Vincent Benét's poem itself, which has been lodged in two teenaged boys' heads for the last fifty-five years.

Steve Martin

Up in the mountains, it's lonesome all the time,
(Sof' win' slewin' thu' the sweet-potato vine.)

Up in the mountains, it's lonesome for a child,
(Whippoorwills a-callin' when the sap runs wild.)

Up in the mountains, mountains in the fog,
Everythin's as lazy as an old houn' dog.

Born in the mountains, never raised a pet,
Don't want nuthin' an' never got it yet.

Born in the mountains, lonesome-born,
Raised runnin' ragged thu' the cockleburrs and corn.

Never knew my pappy, mebbe never should.
Think he was a fiddle made of mountain laurel-wood.

Never had a mammy to teach me pretty-please.
Think she was a whippoorwill, a-skittin' thu' the trees.

Never had a brother ner a whole pair of pants,
But when I start to fiddle, why, yuh got to start to dance!

Listen to my fiddle —
Kingdom Come — Kingdom Come!
Hear the frogs a-chunkin'
"Jug o' rum, Jug o' rum!"

Hear that mountain whippoorwill
be lonesome in the air,
An' I'll tell yuh how I travelled
to the Essex County Fair.

Essex County has a mighty pretty fair,
All the smarty fiddlers from the South come there.

Elbows flyin' as they rosin up the bow
For the First Prize Contest
in the Georgia Fiddlers' Show.

Old Dan Wheeling, with his whiskers in his ears,
King-pin fiddler for nearly twenty years.

Big Tom Sergeant, with his blue wall-eye,
An' Little Jimmy Weezer that can make a fiddle cry.

All sittin' roun', spittin' high an' struttin' proud,
(Listen, little whippoorwill, yuh better bug yore eyes!)

Tun-a-tun-a-tunin' while the jedges told the crowd
Them that got the mostest claps'd win the bestest prize.

Everybody waitin' for the first tweedle-dee,
When in comes a-stumblin' -- hill-billy me!

Bowed right pretty to the jedges an' the rest,
Took a silver dollar from a hole inside my vest,

Plunked it on the table an' said, "There's my callin' card!
An' anyone that licks me -- well, he's got to fiddle hard!"

Old Dan Wheeling, he was laughin' fit to holler,
Little Jimmy Weezer said, "There's one dead dollar!"

Big Tom Sergeant had a yaller-toothy grin,
But I tucked my little whippoorwill
spang underneath my chin,
An' petted it an' tuned it till the jedges said, "Begin!"

Big Tom Sargent was the first in line;
He could fiddle all the bugs off a sweet-potato vine.

He could fiddle down a possum from a mile-high tree,
He could fiddle up a whale from the bottom of the sea.

Yuh could hear hands spankin' till they
spanked each other raw,
When he finished variations on "Turkey in the Straw."

Little Jimmy Weezer was the next to play;
He could fiddle all night, he could fiddle all day.

He could fiddle chills, he could fiddle fever,
He could make a fiddle rustle like a lowland river.

He could make a fiddle croon like a lovin' woman.
An' they clapped like thunder
when he'd finished strummin'.

Then came the ruck of the bob-tailed fiddlers,
The let's-go-easies, the fair-to-middlers.

They got their claps an' they lost their bicker,
An' they all settled back for some more corn-licker.

An' the crowd was tired of their no-count squealing,
When out in the center steps Old Dan Wheeling.

He fiddled high and he fiddled low,
(Listen, little whippoorwill,
yuh got to spread yore wings!)

He fiddled and fiddled with a cherrywood bow,
(Old Dan Wheeling's got bee-honey in his strings).

He fiddled a wind by the lonesome moon,
He fiddled a most almighty tune.

He started fiddling like a ghost.
He ended fiddling like a host.

He fiddled north an' he fiddled south,
He fiddled the heart right out of yore mouth.

He fiddled here an' he fiddled there.
He fiddled salvation everywhere.

When he was finished, the crowd cut loose,
(Whippoorwill, they's rain on yore breast.)
An' I sat there wonderin' "What's the use?"

(Whippoorwill, fly home to yore nest.)
But I stood up pert an' I took my bow,
An' my fiddle went to my shoulder, so.

An' — they wasn't no crowd to get me fazed —
But I was alone where I was raised.

Up in the mountains, so still it makes yuh skeered.
Where God lies sleepin' in his big white beard.

An' I heard the sound of the squirrel in the pine,
An' I heard the earth a-breathin' thu' the long night-time.

They've fiddled the rose, and they've fiddled the thorn,
But they haven't fiddled the mountain-corn.

They've fiddled sinful an' fiddled moral,
But they haven't fiddled the breshwood-laurel.

They've fiddled loud, and they've fiddled still,
But they haven't fiddled the whippoorwill.

I started off with a dump-diddle-dump,
(Oh, hell's broke loose in Georgia!)

Skunk-cabbage growin' by the bee-gum stump.
(Whippoorwill, yo're singin' now!)

My mother was a whippoorwill pert,
My father, he was lazy,

But I'm hell broke loose in a new store shirt
To fiddle all Georgia crazy.

Swing yore partners -- up an' down the middle!
Sashay now -- oh, listen to that fiddle!

Flapjacks flippin' on a red-hot griddle,
An' hell's broke loose,
Hell's broke loose,

Fire on the mountains -- snakes in the grass.
Satan's here a-bilin' -- oh, Lordy, let him pass!

Go down Moses, set my people free;
Pop goes the weasel thu' the old Red Sea!

Jonah sittin' on a hickory-bough,
Up jumps a whale -- an' where's yore prophet now?

Rabbit in the pea-patch, possum in the pot,
Try an' stop my fiddle, now my fiddle's gettin' hot!

Whippoorwill, singin' thu' the mountain hush,
Whippoorwill, shoutin' from the burnin' bush,

Whippoorwill, cryin' in the stable-door,
Sing tonight as yuh never sang before!

Hell's broke loose like a stompin' mountain-shoat,
   Sing till yuh bust the gold in yore throat!

   Hell's broke loose for forty miles aroun'
Bound to stop yore music if yuh don't sing it down.

Sing on the mountains, little whippoorwill,
Sing to the valleys, an' slap 'em with a hill,
For I'm struttin' high as an eagle's quill,

An' hell's broke loose,
Hell's broke loose,
Hell's broke loose in Georgia!

They wasn't a sound when I stopped bowin',
(Whippoorwill, yuh can sing no more.)
But, somewhere or other, the dawn was growin',
(Oh, mountain whippoorwill!)

An' I thought, "I've fiddled all night an' lost,
Yo're a good hill-billy, but yuh've been bossed."
So I went to congratulate old man Dan,

— But he put his fiddle into my han' —
An' then the noise of the crowd began!

John McEuen thought his teenage dream job in Disneyland's Magic Shop at 16 years old was as good as it gets. He and lifelong high- school friend both got that 1963 job (co-worker, Steve Martin). After seeing Missouri bluegrass group The Dillards, John's life headed towards his new dream: make magic with music. His dream became more of a reality than imagined it could be.

In 1971 John initiated the now landmark *Will the Circle be Unbroken** album, hooking Nitty Gritty Dirt Band up with his musical mentors Earl Scruggs and Doc Watson to record; it grew to inviting Mother Maybelle Carter, Jimmy Martin, Roy Acuff, Vassar Clements, Junior Huskey, and Merle Travis for 5 magic hot August days of recording. Now multi-platinum, "Circle" is both the Library of Congress and the Grammy Hall of Fame.

Multi-instrumentalist McEuen (banjo, guitar, mandolin, fiddle) recognized as a founding member and award-winning outstanding performer of the Nitty Gritty Dirt Band, from which he departed at the end of the 50th year anniversary tour Oct. 22, 2017. NGDB was inducted in to Colorado Music Hall of Fame 2015, all covered in his highly praised book *The Life I've Picked*.

McEuen's over 46 albums (7 solo) have earned five platinum and six gold recognition awards, multiple Grammys and nominations, CMA and ACM awards, an Emmy film score nomination, IBMA record of the year award. John's production of *Steve Martin – The Crow* won the 2010 Best Bluegrass Album Grammy. His *The Music of the Wild West* CD- was honored with the *Western Heritage Award*. Other accolades include: Grammy nomination for *String Wizards II*; the *Uncle Dave Macon Award*; 2009 he was inducted in to the *Traditional Country Music Hall of Honor*.

John was inducted to the *American Banjo Museum Hall of Fame*. In 2010, the *Best in the West Award* solo performer - Folk Alliance Organization; McEuen earned the 2013 *Charlie Poole Lifetime Achievement Award*.

Made in Brooklyn, produced by John and David Chesky: Stereophile Magazine's *Record of the Month*; Independent Music Award's *Best Americana Album* in 2018

John's popular Sirius/XM *Acoustic Traveller Show*, now in its 18th year, on The Village channel. Radio Host, author, television show producer, writer, concert promoter, multi-instrumental musician, performer, magician.

"I am grateful that people continue to support what I do, as it allows me to continue making things. I feel like some of my best projects are ahead. So many stories. so many songs, so many notes, so little time!"

Made in the USA
Columbia, SC
05 April 2024

33774030R00024